Thank you!

@LemlemKP

 @lemlemkentibap

"Every child deserves a parent who is willing to fight for them until the end; a superhero who will never give up on them."

Lemlem Kentiba-Paige

KING YOSEF AND HIS SUPERHEROES

LEMLEMKP
BELIEVE

Published by
LemlemKP, LLC.

KING YOSEF
AND HIS
SUPERHEROES

Story by
Lemlem Kentiba-Paige

Illustrations by
Randy Jennings

Mom   King Yosef   Dad

Talking Lilly
(Speech Therapist)

Touching Willow
(Occupational Therapist)

Behavior Sarah
(Applied Behavior Analysis Therapist)

Yosef was a young king. He lived in Miracle Kingdom with his family. This kingdom was filled with beautiful trees, plants, and animals.

This was a day of celebration. It was the young king's second birthday.

Everyone in Miracle Kingdom joined in the celebration. There were games and dancing. Everyone sang "Happy Birthday" to the young king.

Then the king's parents noticed that something was wrong. Yosef had jumped out of his throne and rushed away from the singing. Something was upsetting the king.

"The music is too loud, and it's bothering my ears," the young king said to himself. He tried to tell his mom and dad but could not speak out loud.

Instead, he held his ears, as tears slide down his cheeks. Frustrated, he walked away.

His mom and dad decided to help King Yosef. They tried to teach him different words and sentences using learning activity games, but it was not working.

Mom and Dad encouraged King Yosef every day, giving him plenty of hugs and kisses. "Yosef, you are strong and powerful. One step at a time, we will get there. We love you no matter what," said Mom and Dad. They knew that it was time to call on the other superheroes to help.

Talking Lilly, Behavior Sarah, and Touching Willow got the call from Mom and Dad. They were ready to help King Yosef.

King Yosef was ready to start daycare. He arrived at the daycare and saw kids playing outside.

He was very excited and wanted to play, so he walked towards the playground.

The kids were very excited to see King Yosef as well. They wanted to play with a new friend.

One of the kids said, "Hi, my name is Yarah, what's your name?"

King Yosef wanted to talk to her, but no words came out.

He kept trying and trying, but he couldn't talk. King Yosef became very upset and cried.

In tears, he thought, "I wish I could talk like the other kids."

"How do I start talking? I wish there were someone to help me," King Yosef thought to himself.

Talking Lilly heard his cry and came to the rescue.

"King Yosef, I'm Talking Lilly and I am here to help," she said.

King Yosef couldn't believe it. He was excited and ready to learn how to talk.

Talking Lilly practiced speech with King Yosef every day.
He learned different words and phrases.

She encouraged him every day and gave him breaks and
hugs when needed. She used her special superpowers of
communication to help him.

King Yosef learned words like yes, cookie, yogurt, give me,
under, and many more.

Soon King Yosef was able to use the new words he learned to play with the other kids.

"Thank you for your help, Talking Lilly!" exclaimed King Yosef.

"Remember, you can do anything you set your mind to," said Talking Lilly.

Talking Lilly gave Yosef a big hug, and off she went to help other kids.

King Yosef was happy that he could talk, but he still was not able to fully express himself.

At first, King Yosef repeated what someone else said word-for-word. When mom said, "King Yosef, do you want a cookie?" he replied, "King Yosef, do you want a cookie?" instead of, "Yes, Mom, I want a cookie."

He didn't know how to respond properly during conversations. Out of frustration, he threw down toys.

"I wish I had someone to help me express myself better," King Yosef thought.

Behavior Sarah heard Yosef's frustration and came to his rescue.

"King Yosef, I'm Behavior Sarah. I am here to help you," she said. King Yosef was so excited to see Behavior Sarah.

Behavior Sarah taught him how to have proper conversations and how to deal with his frustration.

She encouraged him every day and gave him breaks and hugs when needed. She used her special superpowers of demonstration, communication, and patience to help him communicate better with others.

Behavior Sarah asked King Yosef, "Do you want a cookie?" King Yosef replied, "Yes, I would like a cookie."

When King Yosef got frustrated, he learned to take deep breaths and repeat a calming word.

King Yosef now could talk and play with the other kids. He could deal with frustrations and have proper conversations.

"Thank you for your help, Behavior Sarah!" said King Yosef.

"Remember, you can do anything you set your mind to," said Behavior Sarah.

Behavior Sarah gave Yosef a big hug, and off she went to help other kids.

The other kids were singing. King Yosef wanted to join, but it was too loud.

King Yosef covered his ears and tiptoed away from the loud singing.

"I wish the loud singing did not bother me and I knew how to walk without tiptoeing," King Yosef said, as he wiped away his tears.

Touching Willow heard King Yosef's cry. She came to his rescue.

"King Yosef, I am Touching Willow, and I am here to help," she said. Yosef was so excited to see Touching Willow.

Touching Willow taught King Yosef how to deal with loud
noises. They did a lot of exercises to help with tiptoeing.

She encouraged him every day and gave him breaks and
hugs when needed. Using her special superpowers, she
taught the young king to walk away from loud voices or to
ask an adult to turn down the radio or TV volume.

She also told everyone to warn him ahead of time about
bells, announcements, fire drills, and loud music.

King Yosef now could listen to music, dance, and have fun.

"Thank you for your help, Touching Willow!" said King Yosef.

"You can do this. You can do anything you set your mind to," said Touching Willow.

Touching Willow gave Yosef a big hug, and off she went to help other kids.

King Yosef was now a happy young boy.

He could speak in full sentences, walk without tiptoeing, and listen to music and dance.

All of the hard work paid off, and the young king did well. He went to school, made new friends, and enjoyed life with his family.

"Life is beautiful, and anything is possible," said King Yosef with a big smile on his face. He lived happily ever after.

Thank you for allowing us to share our story with you. We have been so blessed with a second chance to bond and communicate with our son. We went through three-and-a-half years of nonstop speech, occupational, and applied analysis therapy with our son, Yosef. We lived in our cars running from one therapy session to another. We understand the frustrations that parents like us go through, even though we are on the other side of it now and Yosef has no signs of autism. We are very grateful for every moment we have with Yosef. He is amazing and has a wonderful sense of humor. There is never a dull moment in our house; Yosef keeps us entertained. He has made the biggest footprint on our hearts. I hope you enjoy our son's story and get encouraged. As long as you don't give up, know that there is always hope.

Conversations with King Yosef

Yosef's favorite activities are playing the piano, swimming, reading, playing with LEGO, and spending time with his family.

Yosef was ready to have a sibling around the age of five-and-a-half. He kept asking us every day when we were going to have another child. While I was driving King Yosef home, he started asking me some questions.

Yosef: "Mom, how did you and Daddy meet?"
Mom (very surprised at the questions): "We met at the library."
Yosef: "OK, great. So how did you get married?"
Mom: "We fell in love, Dad asked me to marry him, and we got married."
Yosef: "Did he give you a ring?"
Mom: "Yes, Yosef, he did."
Yosef: "How did you have me?"
Mom (completely caught off guard and not ready to answer the question): "Well, Daddy gave me a special kiss, I got pregnant, and I gave birth to you."
Yosef: "Was I at the wedding?"
Mom: "No, Yosi, you were not."
Yosef: "Oh, I think I was in your stomach at the wedding. I remember; therefore, I was at the wedding."
Mom: "OK, King Yosef."
We got home, and a couple minutes later, Yosef walked up to me and gave me a kiss.
Yosef: "Mom, that was a special kiss, so you can give me a sibling because Dad is taking forever for his special kiss."

We have always taught Yosef about his roots and where his family is from. He knows that I am from East Africa and his dad is an American.

He has always said that he is both East African and American; he has embraced his roots. He loves making Eritrean/Ethiopian coffee with me, enjoys eating Injera (Eritrean/Ethiopian traditional food), and always wants to learn my language. One day, he went to visit his aunt's house and started talking to his cousin, Sewit.

Yosef: "I'm from Africa. My mom was born in Africa; therefore, I was also born in Africa."
Cousin Sewit: "No, Yosi, you were born in Maryland."
Yosef: "Sewit, listen to me, I was born in Africa like my mother. I'm an African."
Cousin Sewit: "No, Yosi, you were born in Ma–"
Yosef: "No, I was born in Africa. You don't know anything about me, and this is the end of the conversation."

Yosef was riding with me as I drove to the grocery store. He was eating an apple and threw what was left out the window.

Mom: "Yosef, you are not supposed to throw trash out of the window."
Yosef: "Mom, it's OK, it was just this time."
Mom: "Yosef, that is not OK, that's called littering."
Yosef: "Oh, Mom, everybody is a critic."

King Yosef asked his Dad if he could use his headphones (White Earbuds).
Dad told Yosef, he was not old enough to use them.
Yosef got some paper towels, and told his Dad he was going to make his own earbuds.
Using the paper towels, he made his own earbuds but they got stuck in his ears.
Yosef came upstairs looking for me and asked to go to the doctor's office to get the paper towels out of his ears.
I told Yosef I would be his doctor and took the paper towels out of his ears.
Yosef gave me a big hug and said, "Thank you mom, you are my doctor, my mother, my cook, you work and have million jobs. You are my Wonder Woman."

★ ABOUT THE AUTHOR ★

LEMLEM KENTIBA-PAIGE was born to Eritrean parents in Addis Ababa, Ethiopia, went to high school in Dallas, Texas, and attended undergraduate and graduate school in Maryland. She is a Senior Cyber Security Engineer and Advisor with a master's degree in Information Technology.

Learn more at lemlemkp.com. Find her on Facebook at facebook.com/lemlemkentibap/ or on Instagram @lemlemkp.

Everything is possible!

I dedicate this book to my son, my husband, my mother, and all of our wonderful family members. We have been through so much as a family, but we overcame every obstacle with the grace and mercy of GOD.

Yosef, my love, my heart, you have worked so hard for over three years to get to where you are, all the reward and the praise belongs to you. We are so very proud to be your parents and to have you in our lives. May GOD continue to bless you in your journey.

To my amazing husband, my best friend and my life partner, you are my rock. I love you for being an amazing father and husband. I could not have done this without your help and support.

Thank you to the most amazing woman in my life, my mother. I don't know where I would be without you. I love you more than life itself. You are an amazing woman of GOD, and I am so thankful for you.

To the grandparents, thank you for being there for us and Yosef. We love you.

I would like to say thank you to all the amazing therapists who worked with my son. I have sat through so many sessions and have seen what you do and how difficult it is to do it day in and day out, but you pushed Yosef and achieved wonderful results. Words can't express how grateful we are for your dedication, hard work, and your kindness toward our child; you will always be part of our lives and stories. Thank you for dedicating your lives to helping kids like my Yosef. You all are amazing superheroes for our little ones.

To all of our family members, and everyone who is in Yosef's life, thank you for being there for him and for supporting him.

We believe early intervention was the key to King Yosef's success.

A very special thank you to Dr. Starr. We are grateful you connected us with the right people to help our son.

If you have any questions, send an email to LemlemKP@gmail.com.

Everything is possible!